It's Robert!

The Triple Rotten Day

Also by Barbara Seuling

The Triple Rotten Day

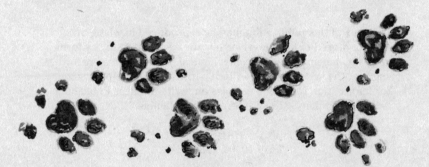

Barbara Seuling

SCHOLASTIC INC.

New York Toronto London Auckland Sydney
Mexico City New Delhi Hong Kong Buenos Aires

ISBN 13: 978-0-545-07191-8
ISBN 10: 0-545-07191-7

Text copyright © 2004 by Barbara Seuling.
Interior illustration, page 33 copyright © 2004 by Paul Brewer.

20   19/0

Printed in the U.S.A.   40

This book is for
Freese, John David, and James Roberts
and for
Christopher, Carter, and Collin Balogh
—B. S.

Contents

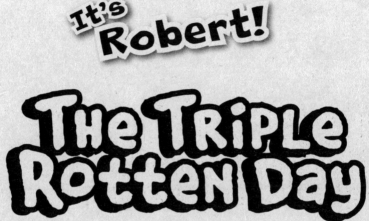

It's Robert!

The Triple Rotten Day

A Bad Start

R-R-RRRRING!

Robert Dorfman awoke from a sound sleep and threw off the covers. Huckleberry, his dog, landed with a thump on the floor.

Robert stumbled over the blanket and the dog to the alarm clock on his dresser to shut it off. He kept the clock far away from his bed so he'd be sure to get up when it rang. Otherwise, he'd just shut it off, turn over, and go back to sleep.

He scratched his dog's head as they made their way to the bathroom. Huckleberry followed him everywhere. Oh, no. The door was locked. Robert knocked. No answer. He knocked again. He pounded on the door.

"What?" came the voice from inside.

"Come on, Charlie. I have to brush my teeth now," Robert called. He was going to be late.

"CHARLIE!" he shouted.

Huckleberry barked.

At last the door opened. Charlie, still wearing his headphones, backed against the wall as Huckleberry moved toward him, still barking.

"Take away your attack dog!" said Charlie.

Robert had to laugh. Attack dog!

Huckleberry was no attack dog. But Robert didn't mind having a dog who helped him out, like he did just now.

After he got dressed, Robert thumped down the stairs and into the kitchen. He let Huckleberry out the door into the backyard.

"Good morning, Rob," said his mom.

"Good morning," he answered, digging the scoop into the dog food bag to fill Huckleberry's bowl. Robert watched his brother slug down a glass of orange juice, then jump up to leave. When Robert got to the table, he reached for the container. He poured, but nothing came out.

"Is there any more orange juice?" he asked.

"I'm afraid not," said his mom. "I'll

put it on the shopping list."

She got up and wrote something on a pad on the refrigerator door, with a pencil that hung from it. "Would you like some grapefruit juice?" she asked.

Robert slumped in his chair. "No, thanks." He hated grapefruit juice. He chewed the edges of a toaster tart around and around until it was just the soft middle. Then he ate that part last, washing it down with milk.

Robert's mom put a brown paper bag next to his plate. "Don't forget your lunch," she reminded him.

"Thanks," he answered, slipping off the chair and into his jacket. He stuffed the lunch bag into his backpack and kissed his mom good-bye.

"See you later," she said. "Have a good day."

"Thanks," said Robert again, slinging the backpack over his shoulder. He waved a good-bye behind him as he ran down the path. He felt grumpy, but he knew things would get better once he met Paul. Every morning Paul Felcher, his best friend, waited for Robert on Paul's corner and they walked to school together. They only took the bus if the weather was bad.

Could it be? Paul wasn't there. But Paul was always there. Unless . . . that must be it. The last time Paul wasn't there was when he was out sick.

Robert dragged his feet, walking the long blocks to school alone. It was as though his sneakers had cement in them.

In the classroom, Robert put his backpack in his space at Table Four, where he sat with Vanessa Nicolini next to him and Paul across from him. Except today. Paul's chair was empty.

Being in Mrs. Bernthal's classroom could usually cheer Robert up, but today he was worried. Mrs. Bernthal had pulled down the monitors chart.

"Class, I'd like your attention, please," said Mrs. Bernthal, as the children settled down. "It's the first of the month and time to choose new monitors. Our present monitors have done an excellent job, so let's give them all a hand," she added. Everyone applauded.

Mrs. Bernthal had the pointer in her hand and aimed it at the first category: plants.

"Who would like to be the plant monitor?" she asked.

Vanessa's hand went up.

"Excellent. Anyone else?" She looked around. Pamela Rose raised her hand.

"Good. Vanessa and Pamela," said Mrs. Bernthal. "You are our new plant monitors. Thank you." She wrote the two names next to plants.

Next, Mrs. Bernthal pointed to clothing closet. Lucy Ritts waved her hand. Brian Hoberman stuck his hand up, too. "Thank you Lucy and Brian." Mrs. Bernthal wrote their names next to clothing closet and went down through the list.

Robert's neck started to itch when Mrs. Bernthal pointed to snake.

Robert had been the snake monitor

and had taken care of Sally, the green ribbon snake, from the day she arrived. Mrs. Bernthal had given Sally to them for being the best class in the whole school. Robert loved Sally. Sally made a little S curve when Robert stroked her back.

"Me! Me!"

He looked around. Lester Willis was standing up and calling out, as usual. Susanne Lee Rodgers and Kevin Kransky also had their hands up.

What was going on? When Sally first came into the class, everyone said the snake was slimy. Some girls, like Melissa Thurm, said she was disgusting. But Robert thought from the first moment he saw her that Sally was beautiful.

Month after month, when new monitors were appointed for the other jobs, nobody wanted to take care of Sally, so Robert kept doing it. He didn't mind. Now, suddenly, everyone was interested.

Susanne Lee was so bossy, she made Robert grind his teeth. She would probably make Sally grind hers, too, if snakes had any teeth.

Kevin Kransky was always biting his nails. Robert was afraid he'd have spit on his hands when he handled Sally. Yuck! Now that would be disgusting!

Lester had once been a bully, but he was better now. That was probably because Robert once helped him with his reading without telling anyone. Still, Lester could play rough. What if he hurt Sally?

"Lester and Susanne Lee, you will be our new snake monitors," said Mrs. Bernthal, adding their names to the chart.

"Cool!" shouted Lester.

Robert slouched in his chair. Mrs. Bernthal continued to assign monitors until all the jobs were filled. Robert got to be one of the window monitors along with Joey Rizzo. It was okay, but it wasn't like being snake monitor.

This day was sure off to a bad start.

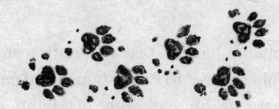

The Bad Fairy

"Class, be sure to take home your math books tonight. Study pages 34 to 39. We're having a test tomorrow."

Robert groaned. Math was his worst subject, unless you counted sports. In sports, at least someone took pity on him now and then and chose him for a team even if they knew he was no good.

Maybe he could get sick, like Paul, and stay home from school! Then he wouldn't have to take the math test. He could go over to Paul's house and catch whatever he had. But his mom and Paul's mom probably wouldn't go for that. Besides, Paul probably had tonsillitis. He'd had that before, and Paul's mom said then that it wasn't catching.

After math, Mrs. Bernthal asked the class to work quietly on their Explorers project.

Robert's diorama was almost done when he turned around suddenly and knocked over the jar of yellow paint.

"Robert!" scolded Susanne Lee Rodgers. "Look what you did!" As if he didn't know without her telling him. Susanne Lee acted like he had ruined her diorama of Robert Peary arriving at the North Pole, but only one little spot of yellow had splashed on the snowy scene. His own diorama, on the other hand, was completely ruined. The whole scene of Balboa, on a cliff looking out over the Pacific Ocean, was covered in yellow paint. He would have to do it all over again. Robert spent the rest of the afternoon cleaning yellow paint off the table, the brushes, the water jar, and himself. He tossed the diorama in the trash.

It was good to hear the bell ring at three o'clock.

When Robert got home, nobody was there except for Huckleberry.

"Hi, Huck," he said, closing the door behind him and dropping his backpack. This was one part of his day that was always good, when the big yellow lab

ran to greet him, wagging his tail, slob-
bering kisses all over him. Robert fell to
his knees to hug the dog.

"You're lucky," he said to his dog,
"that you don't have to go to school.
I had one terrible day today. And I'm
starved." He marched into the kitchen,
Huck prancing along beside him. Robert
saw a note on the refrigerator door.

Oh, no! He had forgotten he had an
appointment with the orthodontist.

On the last visit, Robert thought he
was getting braces like Charlie's. His
brother's braces were red, white, and
blue and were kind of cool.

But Dr. Fargus had told Robert's
mom that Robert was too young for
regular braces. What he needed was a
palate expander. That, he explained,

was a little metal device that would be placed on the roof of Robert's mouth and be attached to his upper teeth with little wires. Each day Robert would have to fit a key into a hole in the metal piece and turn it once. Little by little, that would expand his palate, making more room for his permanent teeth to come in.

That didn't sound cool at all. It sounded like mouth torture. Robert helped himself to a carton of apple juice from the fridge and went outside to the backyard with Huck. He sat on the step by the back door while Huck raced around the yard, sniffing along the fence.

"Yeah, I know those squirrels drive you crazy," said Robert. "They come in the yard just to tease you and then they leave before you get here." Robert drank his juice as he watched Huck sniff frantically at the roots of the apple tree.

Finally, Huck came over and lay down at Robert's feet.

"Hey, Huck. Do you think it's possible that a bad fairy touched me with her wand this morning and now she won't leave me alone?"

Huck rolled over on his back.

"I guess you don't believe in fairies," Robert said, rubbing the dog's belly. But he wasn't sure about them himself. SOMETHING was giving him all this bad luck.

Mouth Torture

Robert sat in the chair in Dr. Fargus's office, staring at all the equipment around him. If he wasn't sitting there, he'd probably think all this stuff was cool. It looked like something out of a creepy science-fiction movie.

"Open wide," said Dr. Fargus, leaning over him. Dr. Fargus wore a white coat and thick glasses, which made him look like a mad scientist. Robert dropped his mouth open. He felt the chair tilt back as Dr. Fargus pumped the pedal with his foot.

Dr. Fargus took a small metal piece from the tray next to the chair and put it in Robert's mouth. It felt cold against the roof of his mouth. Robert tried to swallow, but he couldn't.

"Smdffssst," he said. That was supposed to be "I have to swallow," but he couldn't form the words with his mouth wide open and a metal contraption in the way. Dr. Fargus hung a long tube with a bent top over his lower teeth.

"I'll be done in a minute," said Dr. Fargus. "This drain will take care of the excess saliva that accumulates." The little tube sucked up Robert's spit with a slurping sound.

Dr. Fargus pushed and tapped and

poked around in his mouth, stopping now and again to put one tool down and pick up another.

Robert wondered if Charlie had to go through all this to have his braces fitted, and if he thought it was weird, too. He stared at the wall with Dr. Fargus's certificates from dental school. He stared at the chest with a gazillion drawers in it and wondered what was in each one. He studied the light that was shining down on him.

He studied Dr. Fargus's face. The doctor looked a little like Sir Mordred, the Black Knight, in a horror movie Robert had seen recently. He noticed that there were hairs growing in his nose.

"Ah, that's a good fit," Dr. Fargus said,

finally, as he stood up. He removed the sucking tube. "Close your mouth slowly and see how that feels."

It felt as though there was a big metal hockey puck stuck on the roof of his mouth. He ran his tongue over it and around the wires that held the piece onto his teeth on both sides.

"How does that feel?" asked Dr. Fargus.

"Ith theels thlunnee," Robert said, as spit trickled down his chin.

"It will feel uncomfortable at first," said Dr. Fargus, handing him a tissue. "Your mouth will probably feel sore for two or three days, until you get used to it." He turned to Robert's mom. "You can give him ibuprofen if he needs it," he said.

"Can he eat regular food?" asked his mom.

"Have him eat soft foods for the first few days," the doctor answered.

Robert felt like he wasn't even in the room as his mom and the doctor talked to each other over him.

"He will also have some trouble speaking . . ." said Dr. Fargus.

No kidding, thought Robert.

"Until he's used to having the palate expander in his mouth," the doctor continued. "But he will get used to it, and that will improve over time."

Wrong! He would NEVER get used to it, Robert decided.

Dr. Fargus smiled. "That's it, young man. You're done." He pumped the chair upright, and Robert slid out. He kept his mouth closed tight. He was not going to make a fool of himself drooling again in front of Dr. Fargus and his mom.

Dr. Fargus pulled a sheet of paper off his desk in the next room and handed it to Robert's mom. "This will explain about eating and speaking and cleaning the palate expander." He put his arm around Robert's shoulders as he walked them out the door.

"So," said Dr. Fargus, "you're on your way to having nice, straight permanent teeth. Doesn't that sound good?"

Robert just grunted. Right now, crooked teeth didn't sound half bad. In Robert's mind, Dr. Fargus had become the evil Sir Mordred, and his office was the torture chamber in an ancient dungeon.

Baby Food

Robert sat on his beanbag chair, picking at a scab on his elbow. His mouth was sore, and his tongue was tired from feeling around the metal piece and the wires all day. He couldn't help it. He wished he could pry the thing off, but it was cemented in.

"Rob, dinner's ready," called his mom from downstairs.

Rats. He had forgotten about dinner. Suddenly, the thought of food made him realize how hungry he was. He got up and went downstairs, thump, thump, thump. On his plate he saw three little piles. Robert had forgotten Dr. Fargus had said he wouldn't be able to chew anything at first, so he'd have to eat soft food.

His mom had given him cottage cheese, mashed potatoes with gravy, and carrots that she had put through the blender.

"That looks like baby food," said Charlie.

Robert stared into his plate. He tried to ignore his brother, who loved to tease him. He took a spoonful of cottage cheese.

It tasted all right, but it got stuck around the wires. He used his tongue to get it loose.

Robert didn't look up, but he just knew Charlie was waiting for an opportunity to laugh at him. He stabbed his fork into the mountain of mashed potatoes.

"So how is it going, Tiger?" asked his dad. Looking up, Robert forgot and started to answer, but when he opened his mouth to speak, he drooled. He quickly wiped his mouth with his napkin but Charlie had seen it and was howling with laughter.

"Charlie, that's enough!" said Robert's mom, but Charlie didn't stop.

"Charlie, leave the table," commanded his dad.

Charlie left, but he was still shaking with laughter.

Robert wished he could disappear

under the mound of mashed potatoes. "May I be ethcused?" he asked, slowly and carefully, so he didn't dribble down his chin. His mom looked at him sympathetically.

"Yes, you may," she said.

Robert slid off his chair and ran upstairs, Huckleberry at his heels. He closed the door to his room and flopped down on his bed, sniffling quietly into his pillow. Huckleberry leaped up next to him and licked Robert's ear. Robert couldn't hold it in any longer and cried, burying his face in Huckleberry's fur.

Paul had once said everyone had a rotten day now and then, when a lot of things seemed to go wrong, but once in a while a person could have a streak of bad things happen and it could be a double rotten day. Well, this was even worse than that. It was a triple rotten day. Maybe it would even go in the Guinness Book of World Records.

He got up and went to the telephone on the upstairs landing. He had to talk to Paul.

"Hello?" It was Paul's mom.

"Hi, Mrs. Felcher. It'th Robert. Can I thpeak to Paul, pleathe?" Oops. He should have said "May I."

"Oh, Robert, I know Paul would love to talk to you, but his throat is so sore, I don't think he should talk at all."

"Oh," said Robert. "Okay." He hoped he didn't sound too disappointed.

"I'll tell Paul you called," said Mrs. Felcher.

"Thankth," said Robert. He hung up

the phone and went back to his room.

Now he was having a triple rotten day and he couldn't even tell his best friend about it.

Loose Wire

The next day, Paul was still not back in school. Robert sat alone at lunch. He didn't want anyone else to see him drooling or eating baby food.

He opened his brown lunch bag and pulled out a plastic container instead of a sandwich baggie. It was yogurt. Strawberry yogurt. It tasted all right, but Robert wished he had a regular old salami sandwich like the ones he was used to. There were no cookies in the bag—just a nice, soft banana. Charlie was right. He was eating baby food.

After washing everything down with milk, Robert felt around his mouth with his tongue. Dr. Fargus had told him not to play around with the device, to try to keep his tongue off it. How could he do that? His tongue wouldn't stay still.

He emptied his tray into the trash barrel and went outside. Some kids were playing ball in the school yard, others were talking. Robert didn't feel like doing either. He went back inside and upstairs to his classroom. Mrs. Bernthal had given him permission to go up to the classroom by himself on his lunch hour to work in the class library.

The room was empty and quiet.

Robert walked over to the bookcases that made up the class library and started to straighten up the books. He glanced over at Sally's tank, sitting on top of the supply cabinets.

Robert walked over and took the top off Sally's tank. "Hi," he said. He reached in and gently stroked her beautiful green body. Sally squiggled into an S curve. Robert didn't have to say a word. Sally was happy, and Robert was happy just being there with Sally again.

He knew it would sound silly to anyone else, but Robert believed Sally understood when he felt sad, or lonely, or happy. She was his third best friend. Paul was his first, Huck was his second, and Sally was his third. Robert kept that to himself.

Robert stayed with Sally, stroking her now and then, until the class and Mrs. Bernthal came back.

"Hey, what are you doing here?" said Lester, coming over to the snake tank.

"Nothing," said Robert.

"Well, you're not the monitor anymore," said Lester. "We get to take care of her now."

Robert swallowed hard. That's what he'd been afraid of.

During Silent Reading, Robert could hardly concentrate on the story in his book. He caught himself several times rolling his tongue around in his mouth.

Wait. Something felt different. One of the wires seemed to be a little loose. His mom would not be happy about that. Now his tongue was going crazy, feeling around that loose wire.

At last, school was over. He had one tired tongue. All day, he had struggled with making his tongue behave, but he just couldn't help himself. The wire was even looser by the end of the day.

Robert let himself into the house with his key, because no one was home except Huckleberry. The big yellow dog greeted him, as always, with a wildly wagging tail.

In the kitchen, Robert found another Post-it on the fridge.

Rob—
Doing errands.
Back around 3:30.
Mom

Robert looked in the fridge and found pudding cups. Butterscotch—his favorite. He flopped on the sofa in the living room to eat his snack. Huckleberry curled up at his feet.

Robert tried not to wiggle the loose wire anymore, but with the last spoonful of pudding, he felt it come off. He took out the wire, brought it to the kitchen, and rinsed it off.

Back in the living room, he put it on the coffee table to show his mom.

What would she do? He'd know soon enough, when she came home.

"Come on, Huck," he called to Huck, picking up a tennis ball. "Let's play some catch." Huck followed him out the back door and into the yard.

This was the best part of the day.

School was over, and Robert could play with Huck. They both ran around the yard, throwing the ball and catching it, chasing each other, wrestling in the grass.

Huck ran to a corner of the yard and started digging.

"Give up, Huck," said Robert. "There's no squirrel there. It's just the smell of a squirrel."

Huck looked up at him, dirt on his nose, then went back to digging some more, dirt flying everywhere. Suddenly, he grabbed something and ran over to Robert with it.

"Yuck!" said Robert. "That's gross." It was a bone covered with yucky stuff. When they went into the house, Robert made Huck leave the bone outside. The dog bounded into the living room.

"Wait!" called Robert, but it was too late. Huck had tracked mud in from all that digging.

Robert grabbed Huck by the collar and led him to the kitchen, where he filled a basin with water and washed the rest of the mud off Huck's paws.

The living room was still a mess, and his mom would be home any minute. He pulled the hand vacuum cleaner off the wall in the broom closet and cleaned up the best he could.

He had just put the vacuum cleaner away when his mom came in.

"Hi, Robbie," she said.

"Hi, Mom."

"Was today any better?" she asked.

Robert had almost forgotten. Playing

with Huck, he had not even thought about the metal piece in his mouth, or the broken wire!

"It was okay. But . . . um . . . a wire came loose," he said.

"Really?" His mother sounded worried. "Is it just loose or did it come out?"

"It was loose first," he said, "and then it came off." He didn't mention that he was wiggling it with his tongue all day.

"Where is it?" his mom asked.

"I put it on the coffee table," he said. He went over to the table to show her. Huck was standing there.

The wire was gone.

Robert got down on his hands and knees and searched the carpet. Huck thought he was playing and came close to nuzzle Robert.

"No, Huck," Robert said. "Not now." He turned around. "Mom, it was here. Honest. It's not here now."

His mom looked worried. "Are you sure you didn't swallow it?"

"What? No, I'm sure. It came out," he said. "I washed it off and put it on the coffee table."

Robert saw his mom's expression change as she looked at Huckleberry. Robert knew right away what his mom was thinking. Huck was right where the wire had been. Could he have eaten it? Robert felt as though someone had hit him in the stomach.

"What'll we do?" he asked in a squeaky voice.

"I'll call the vet," his mom said, going

to the telephone.

A minute later, she was whisking them both out the door and into her car. "We have to take him in right away, for an X-ray," she explained. "If he swallowed it, it will show up. And if it didn't get to his stomach yet, they can get it out with a scope."

"What's a scope?" Robert was beginning to panic.

"It's something they can put down his throat to find it and pull it out before it goes into his intestine, where it could get caught."

"Won't that hurt?" he asked.

"No," said his mom, easing the car out of the driveway. "They'll give him something to put him out first," said his mom. "He won't feel a thing."

Emergency!

At the vet's office, Huck wagged his tail as Dr. Treat came out to greet him.

"Don't worry," he said. "This should be quick." Dr. Treat took Huck to the back. Robert wished he could follow him, but he stayed next to his mom in the waiting room.

As he sat with his mom in the waiting room, he thought about his triple rotten day. It was now two days. Did it have a new name when it went into a second day? He must be nearing a record now.

About twenty minutes later, Dr. Treat came out with Huck walking slowly behind him. "You have nothing to worry about," he said. "Huckleberry didn't swallow anything he shouldn't have. He's still drowsy from the medication, but he'll be fine in a few minutes."

Robert knelt down on the floor and gave Huck a big hug, even if Huck was still too groggy to appreciate it.

"Next we have to see Dr. Fargus," said Robert's mom.

Now that Huckleberry was okay, his mom was back on track.

They got in the car, with Huckleberry in the backseat. Huck loved the car. He was awake now, and already had his head out the window. Robert wished they could just go home and play.

"Mom, do I really have to do this?" asked Robert.

"Yes, I'm afraid so," said his mom. "Don't you want strong, straight teeth?"

"I guess so," said Robert, who really hadn't thought much about his teeth. He knew he had to brush and floss to keep his teeth healthy, and he didn't mind that—he did that all the time. But this . . . this . . . mouth torture was something else.

"But what if Huck had swallowed the wire? Or if I had? It can be dangerous."

"You have a point," said his mom, "and I plan to speak to Dr. Fargus about that. I'd like him to explain to me how we can prevent this from happening again."

"Are you mad at me for making the wire come out?" asked Robert.

His mom smiled. "No, I'm not mad at you, Robbie," she said. "Asking you not to wiggle your tongue around the palate expander is like asking you not to think of elephants."

"What do you mean?"

"Well, what happens when I say 'Don't think about elephants'?"

"Um . . . I . . . think about elephants," said Robert.

"The minute your attention is called to something, it's in your mind, right on the surface. You can't NOT think of it," his mom said.

Robert smiled. "That's cool."

"Well, you probably would have wiggled the wire, anyway," said his mom. "It's human nature to be curious, especially when something is not the way it usually is."

Robert was relieved that his mom understood. But would Dr. Fargus?

A Mess

Robert climbed into the orthodontist's chair once again.

Dr. Fargus wasn't upset. He talked to Robert as he removed the palate expander from his mouth. It took some tapping to loosen it, but that wasn't bad.

"I'm sorry this has been so uncomfortable for you," he said. He sounded like he meant it.

"Aaa ooo," said Robert, his mouth wide.

Dr. Fargus held up the palate expander. "You get a break for a few days, young man, while I order a new one," he said.

Robert smiled at being called a young man. It made him feel good.

Dr. Fargus motioned for Robert to get down from the chair. "I'll call you when it's ready," he said to Robert's mom. He looked at Robert again. "Meanwhile, you can eat anything you like."

"Yes!" said Robert, visions of hamburgers floating in his head.

He didn't even have to tell his mom. On the way home, they stopped at the store to pick up hamburger meat and his favorite chocolate-covered jelly cookies. She also bought salami for his lunch.

"Rob, I'm still wondering what happened to that wire," said his mom as they drove the rest of the way home. "If it's around, there's still the possibility that Huck will find it and swallow it."

Robert searched his brain for ideas about where the wire could be. He had checked his pockets and the carpet around the table where the wire had been. He even checked where he had cleaned up Huck's muddy footprints.

The footprints! Of course!

"Mom!"

"What is it?"

"I know where the wire is."

"Really? Where?"

Robert told his mom about the digging and the yucky bone and the muddy footprints and using the hand vacuum cleaner. "I bet Huck brushed the wire onto the floor with his tail, and I vacuumed it up by mistake."

"There's only one way to find out," said his mom, laughing.

When they got home, Robert grabbed the hand vacuum cleaner and was opening it when his mom said, "Better take that outside."

It was a tiny bit too late. Dirt flew out. Robert clamped it back together and took it out to the backyard. Huck followed him. A moment later, his mom came after them.

"Here," she said, handing him some newspapers and a pair of rubber gloves. "These will help."

Robert slowly opened the vacuum cleaner over the newspaper. Even though most of the dirt fell out on the newspaper, dust flew into the air. Huck sneezed and backed away.

Robert pulled on the rubber gloves. Bit by bit, he sifted through the dirt, looking for the wire, which was no bigger than a paper clip. The rubber gloves did help, but what he needed was a clothespin for his nose!

"Here it is!" he shouted at last.

His mom came out to see. "Good work, Rob," she said. She took the wire from him. "I'll put this in a safe place. Meanwhile, clean up this mess before your father gets home."

Robert rolled up the newspaper and put it in the trash. He rinsed off the rubber gloves and left them by the sink to dry.

His mom looked pleased. "You solved the mystery of the missing wire. You'd make a good detective."

"Maybe," Robert answered, "but I'd rather be an orthodontist."

"Really?" said his mom. "I thought you wanted to work with animals."

"I do. But I want to be like Dr. Fargus. Do you think animals need palate expanders or retainers?" Robert pictured him opening Huck's mouth to examine him for a palate expander.

Robert's mom laughed. "I don't know. That's an interesting idea."

Robert laughed, too. Sometimes he cracked himself up.

Hamburger Again

Dinner was late because of all the excitement, but Robert didn't mind. They were having hamburgers. He drooled, but this time it was for the juicy burger on his plate.

"Robert, for the next few days, while you can still eat normally, we'll eat your favorite foods."

"Even takeout?" he asked.

"Even takeout," said his mom.

"Cool!" said Charlie, giving Robert a

high five. Sometimes Robert and Charlie saw eye to eye on things. They both knew their mom was not a great cook, and take-out meant they didn't have to eat her cooking.

"Mom?"

"Yes, Rob?"

"I decided the palate expander is probably a good thing, once you get past the drooling and stuff."

His mom looked surprised. "I'm glad to hear it, Rob. But what makes you say that?"

"Dr. Fargus told me he was going to invent a better palate expander one day so kids could eat hamburgers and other good stuff without a problem."

"Ah," said Robert's mom. "That would be good."

"Yeah." Robert smiled.

BAM! Something made a loud pop in the kitchen.

Robert's mom jumped up and ran to the oven. She opened the door, and lots of smoke billowed out.

"Oh, no!" she exclaimed.

"What happened?" asked Mr. Dorfman, who had run in after her.

"My apple pie," said his mom. "It exploded!"

Robert looked at Charlie, and Charlie looked at Robert. They couldn't help it—they both burst out laughing.

"It isn't funny!" their mom wailed. "I thought it would be nice to have apple pie with dinner tonight, in honor of Rob's being able to eat real food again."

Robert tried to stop laughing. That was really nice of his mom. But everyone knew about her cooking. Maybe it was just as well it exploded.

Huck went over to the oven, sniffing.

"Well, I guess Huckleberry will have what's left of the pie."

"See? You've made someone very happy with your pie," said Robert's dad.

Mrs. Dorfman had a strange look on her face. Robert and Charlie snickered again.

"Mom, didn't you buy some chocolate-covered jelly cookies today?" asked Robert.

"Yes, I did. . . ."

"Then we can have those for dessert," said Robert, jumping up to get them.

"Yeah," said Charlie. "Everyone likes chocolate-covered jelly cookies. Right, Dad?"

Mr. Dorfman nodded. "The boy has a good point," he said.

"And it isn't like we're starving," said Robert. His mom always made him feel good about his disasters. Maybe he could help her now with hers.

"You're all being very nice," said Robert's mom, returning to the table with the coffeepot. She poured a cup for Robert's dad and another for herself. "Tomorrow, we'll have apple pie for dessert, I promise."

Charlie let out a groan. Robert kicked him under the table. He hoped his mom didn't hear it.

"I'll pick one up from the bakery," his

mom added.

"Great!" they all answered at once.

After dinner, Robert went upstairs to his room to do his homework. Huck was there at his side.

"Hey," said Robert, patting the dog. "I get to choose what we have for dinner tomorrow night, and I choose pepperoni pizza." Huck danced around and found one of his toys, swinging it from his mouth, jawing it so the squeaker squeaked.

"Huck, you know what I think?"

Huckleberry stopping swinging the goose and stood there staring up at Robert.

"I think my triple rotten day is over."

Paul's Back

Robert sprang out of bed the next morning, three minutes before the alarm was set to go off.

"Yes!" he said, shutting off the alarm button.

Sure enough, Paul was back on his corner when Robert got there.

"Boy, am I glad to see you!" said Robert, running up to him, his backpack bouncing.

"Yeah, me too," said Paul. He picked

up his backpack from the sidewalk. "It was beginning to be a little boring. No, a LOT boring."

"I'm talking about worse than boring," said Robert. "I'm talking about a bad day, rotten luck, horrible, no good, hope-it-never-happens-again streak of bad things happening."

"Really? What happened?"

Robert told him. He started with that first morning when Charlie hogged the bathroom, then all the things that went wrong that day, including having the palate expander put in, and on through the next day, when the wire came loose and he lost it and they thought Huck had swallowed it. He told him about the X-ray, and Dr. Fargus, and his sore mouth. He told Paul how he tried to call him, but his mom said Paul's throat was sore and he couldn't talk.

"I'm sorry," said Paul.

"That's okay," said Robert. "I know you were sick. It's just that it was a triple rotten day, and I didn't have anyone to talk to about it." He walked along with new energy in every step. "I thought I'd make a new record and get in the Guinness Book of World Records," he finished.

"I don't think you had a triple rotten day," said Paul finally.

"Really?" Robert slowed down a bit. He couldn't imagine why not. It seemed terrible at the time. Maybe being out sick was worse? How could he be so dumb? He hadn't even asked Paul how he felt.

"Oh. Hey. How are you feeling?" he asked.

"I'm fine," said Paul. "Thanks. I think you had more than a triple rotten day," he added.

"Really?" What could be worse than a triple rotten day? Robert was amazed. Maybe he made a record after all.

Paul nodded. Then he said, "Well, to start with, it was not a day, it was two days. But then—think about it. You thought Huck had swallowed a wire, but found out he was okay. That was good."

Robert let that sink in.

"Then, the wire came loose, but it made Dr. Fargus get you a new, better palate expander."

Robert hadn't seen it that way, but

Paul was right. That was also a good thing.

"And finally," said Paul, "the evil Sir Mordred the Black Knight turned into your hero."

Robert sighed. Paul could always see things in a way that made him feel better.

"It was kind of neat there for a while, thinking of getting into the Guinness Book of World Records," said Robert.

"If you're going to get into the Guinness Book of World Records," said Paul, "you ought to pick something that's more fun than having bad luck."

"Yeah. Like having the most dogs," said Robert.

"Or drawing the most pictures," said Paul.

"Or eating the most chocolate-covered jelly cookies," said Robert.

"Or riding a bike the longest," said Paul.

It was so good to have Paul back. The walk to school had been so long and boring without him.

In the classroom, Robert saw Susanne Lee and Lester at Sally's tank.

"Oh, yeah," he said to Paul as they put their backpacks on their table. "Mrs. Bernthal chose new monitors. Sally got Susanne Lee and Lester."

Paul spun around. "No way!" he said.

"Way," said Robert. He couldn't resist going over for a look. Paul followed him.

"Hello, Robert," said Susanne Lee

sweetly. "Have you come to see your girlfriend?"

What made Susanne Lee such a jerk? Everyone knew she was the smartest one in the class. But did she always have to act like she owned everything?

"I just came to see if Sally is still alive," said Robert. "I figure she might have died of fright when you came near her."

"You're pitiful," Susanne Lee said and walked off toward her desk, her hair bouncing. Robert didn't care. She made him mad sometimes.

"What's that in Sally's tank?" asked Paul.

It was a big rock.

Lester came over. "Yo, Robert," he said.

"Who put that rock in there?" asked Robert.

"I did," said Lester. "It's a hot rock. We got it so Sally would always be warm. You know how bad cold is for snakes."

"Cool," said Robert. He had seen hot rocks at the pet store. He smiled as he remembered the scary time Sally got loose over a cold winter weekend. He had thought she might die, but the custodian saw her and brought her down to the boiler room to keep warm.

"That's a good idea," Robert said, touching the hot rock with his finger. Maybe Lester wasn't such a bad snake monitor after all.

"Susanne Lee bought it," Lester added.

Susanne Lee? Robert couldn't believe it. As he and Paul walked back to their table, he thought about what he'd said to Susanne Lee. He knew he ought to apologize.

"I'll be right back," he said to Paul. He walked over to Susanne Lee at the next table. "That was nice," he said finally.

Susanne Lee looked around at him.

"The hot rock for Sally," he said.

"Thanks," she said. There was a pause. "You're not the only one who likes Sally, you know."

Robert's neck itched. He felt his cheeks get hot. "Yeah. I didn't know." He went back to his table and sat down.

Things sure had a way of working out in the most unexpected ways. Who would have ever thought that Susanne

Lee would like Sally the snake? Or that Lester would be so gentle with her?

This was a peculiar day. After the last two days, it seemed to fly by.

When school was over, Robert and Paul started the long walk home.

"I've been thinking," said Paul. "What about trying the most flavors of ice cream?"

"You mean for getting into the Guinness Book of World Records?" asked Robert.

Paul nodded. "My mom always has ice cream around because of my tonsillitis. She says it's good for my throat. We could start there."

"Okay," said Robert. "I have to eat soft food when I get my new palate expander. Ice cream is soft. I can ask for a different flavor every night."

"Cool."

"I once had banana cinnamon swirl," said Robert.

"I had mango," answered Paul.

"I have to call my mother to tell her I'm at your house."

"Yeah."

They ran the rest of the way to Paul's house, eager to get started.

BARBARA SEULING is a well-known author of fiction and nonfiction books for children, including several books about Robert. She divides her time between New York City and Vermont.